The Long Iron Tracks

The Long Iron Tracks

A. W. Nelson

RESOURCE *Publications* • Eugene, Oregon

THE LONG IRON TRACKS

Resource Publications
An Imprint of Wipf and Stock Publishers
199 W. 8th Ave., Suite 3
Eugene, OR 97401

www.wipfandstock.com

PAPERBACK ISBN: 978-1-7252-7800-4
HARDCOVER ISBN: 978-1-7252-7796-0
EBOOK ISBN: 978-1-7252-7801-1

To the one who found me . . .

Contents

Preface

The idea for this story came to me one morning before work a couple years ago, during a time when I was doing everything I could to avoid listening to the voice of wisdom inside of me. I was having trouble at my job (which was the first one I ever had out of college) and doubting my own value very much when God posed the question to me internally, "Why are you so sad, Andy?". When you read that question, you must not think it sounds like a parent asking their kid why they are crying after having just witnessed them fall of their bike from the kitchen window. In that case, the parent is providing their child with the opportunity to express their pain. This "why" was a direct question demanding a direct answer, almost like a police officer demanding to know why you were speeding 15 mph. over the limit. I of course, much like those who get pulled over for speeding, knew very well *why* I was sad and simply did not want to come to terms with the reality that my own life was turning out to be quite different than I had planned. In short, I wasn't doing the things I ought to and it was soul killing.

But God continued to press me. I felt strongly that he was asking me to set time aside to write and to listen. In those days, my whole job was corporate writing, and I would come home every day burnt and exhausted and in no mode to sit and think deeply. God fired back that I should then get up early, when my mind was still fresh. In horror, I thought of much more tired I might be once I got even less sleep. However, the notion that God was suggesting this to me in large part because it was exactly what would help me to feel less tired came to rest on me like a brick—right in the center of my chest. I wanted to shut my ears and pretend I had not heard that voice.

At the same moment that I was tempted to ignore the burning supposition being hurled like a spear straight into the middle of my heart, another voice came quietly into the scene. "Why don't you just try it? You really *are* unhappy enough as it is." Grumblings and moaning soon followed this voice but quickly died away as I begrudgingly accepted the challenge. It was a curiosity to me, that I might in fact find joy in listening to the voice of God. I didn't know it at the time, but I was desperate for change. So, I purchased a commentary on the book of Daniel, and began showing up to work an hour earlier so that I could sit and read and write.

The first few days were hard, and I wanted to stop. Somehow or another, I kept at it; and, as I persisted, I noticed that the nature of my thoughts began to change. Chiefly, I found that my imagination was growing, and I started to picture in my mind how the words that I read, both in the Bible and in that commentary on Daniel, were relevant to my day to day. I became insatiable in my desire to read and learn more. It got to the point where I didn't want to stop reading and writing and start my actual job. Just around that time I actually saw the image of the Long Iron Tracks in my mind and myself as the dusty engine sitting there waiting. I whipped out my laptop and began to write. What came out after about 30 minutes of furious typing was the beginning of this book. I was so moved by the image that I continued the day after and spent the rest of the year writing on and off to finish it.

What is most amazing to me now, having finished the book, is the realization that I never intended to write it. God knew that I needed to. Much of the narrative that follows is a direct reflection of the thoughts and emotions that I had as I was undergoing a process of transformation that would pull me out of the tireless grip of monotony and boredom into a life full of color and meaning. It was all already there; I simply lacked the eyes to see it and was all too ready to believe in my fears. When I started, I had little idea that anyone would pick up my writing and be interested in reading the fantastical images that had come to me in the quiet dark of the morning. Really, I don't think that was the point. I simply wouldn't be the person I ought to be if I had not been so relentlessly pursued by the one who loves us the most.

The reader may take note of the curious beginning of this novel which happens quite suddenly and with little explanation. Know that this hard start is how God decided to drop me in the deep end and is followed by an adventure of discovery whereby the intention behind such a jarring action is explained. Additionally, I must admit that the story was written almost entirely in chronological order. The ending was not planned, it is simply the point in which my imagination ceased to produce a coherent story. As a writer and rabid reader of fiction, I can say that most stories do *not* happen in this way. The author usually likes to plan the plot out beforehand which I did not do. I don't mean to suggest that I sat down and received a divine image either, though. While I consider God to be the architect of this story, there is certain to be fallible images contained within. My only response to this is that one of the chief joys of life is returning unexpectedly to the realization that God is so much bigger than you previously thought. I expect this to be no different.

1

Asleep, Awake, and across a Bridge

As I stood upon the earth, my feet planted in the soil, I felt a great wind sweeping over me. I had risen in the morning to watch the sunrise, looking toward the East with great anticipation. It was thus when—to my surprise—from behind, a rushing came. It started soft and gentle but soon picked up, causing my hair to dance as it pressed over me. I turned to face it, moving with ease as its spirit enveloped me. When it did, my heart began to burn. I saw myself as an old and rusted steam engine silent and sleeping on a long iron track which lead out far beyond my sight. Then, with the pressing of the wind and the rising of the sun, an Engineer did cheerfully appear from inside a small shack that stood beside the tracks.

The Engineer whistled brightly as he walked beside my frame, inspecting the rust on my wheels. Curiosity bubbled up within me as I watched him walk across the ground beside the tracks, though I did not call out to him (as the rust prevented me from doing so). Several minutes were spent in careful observation; I of he and he of me, before the Engineer finally completed his task and turned to address me.

"Mind if I come in for a look?" he asked, doffing his cap politely.

As this was the first time he spoke, I was surprised when I felt a sudden familiarity in his voice. With no notion of my own origin,

I couldn't say why I felt this way, but an eagerness to allow him to continue his work welled up from within me and I nodded to him my agreement. Then, quick as a deer, he gripped the sides of my frame and jumped up into the cabin space—the typical perch for one doing an Engineer's work. The inside of the cabin, though not rusted like the outside of my frame, was filled with dust which the Engineer began to clean. There he sat, for hours at a time, hunching himself over while wiping everything with a rag he kept in his pocket. Upon further inspection, one could see the rag was worn and weathered, not unlike the man himself. Creases licked the edges of a taut and measured gaze that produced an effect in me not unlike when one stands on the railing of a footbridge and gazes into the slow-moving water it crosses. It was the look of someone who has long been at the same methodical work and, while not drained spiritually, has nevertheless experienced the natural result of toiling away. After allowing the cabin to air out and breathe once again, he began flipping switches, testing their connections to see which were faulty and might need replacing. I could hear him scribbling with an old wooden pencil that left bits of charcoal on his fingers and a large smudge on the side of his right hand as he jotted down things of note. After a while, he jumped back outside and onto the ground again.

"One moment while I grab something," he said politely as he walked back to the small shack by the tracks. Time passed slowly until he emerged carrying a large shovel across his shoulders. He then returned and began looking into the coal car attached directly to my engine.

"You are empty, my friend!" he exclaimed, shaking his head upon inspection. "No wonder you are stuck here!"

He then called out to his firemen for assistance. Soon they appeared hauling numerous bags of coal which they poured into my coal car at the direction of the Engineer who was now standing once again in the cabin of my frame. In minutes my coal car was full to the brim.

"That's enough!" the Engineer said with a clap of his hands. "I'll take it from here!"

Following his instructions, the firemen zipped up their bags and returned cheerfully to their station. The Engineer then reached into his pocket and pulled out a matchbox. He opened it carefully, withdrawing a single match which he held in his smudged hand. With his free limb, he wrested open the door to my furnace which was cold, dark, and full of ashes. Then with a quick strike across his overalls the match was brought to life as a tiny flame. He hovered for just a moment beside the dusty aperture; the air was so still the flame did not quiver. I assumed he was preparing to light the furnace, but with what material I had no idea.

"Are you ready?" he asked with a low voice. In my frozen state I was just able to stifle out a nervous laugh which sent up a bit of ash out of the furnace and onto the Engineer's clean brow. "I'll take that as a yes!" he said, grinning through the dust.

Then, to my surprise, the Engineer turned away from my open hearth toward the coal car and flicked the tiny match into it, igniting all the coals at once! He then grabbed the shovel he had brought and started to fill the open hearth with the hot coals. I sputtered and coughed violently as the heat caused the old ashes to exit through my smokestack, billowing out in thick black clouds that smelled most foul. Then I, once a cold and dormant locomotive, did awaken with a low rumble. With the shovel, wider than my furnace door, he continued to fling in great heaps of the coal which were already ablaze. In the confined space, the fire soon engulfed my old hearth, and I felt my rusted wheels begin to turn. Following a great lurch, we started down the track. I traversed slowly at first, feeling the strain of the train behind me. I groaned horribly looking back behind me where I saw a long train of cars. I knew at once that these were my burdens, coupled together in a long line stretching out far behind me. Anyone who has gone for months without exercising and then suddenly decides to run a mile will understand how I felt in the moment. If I had been capable of retching in that state, I doubtless would have done so but as a steam engine I simply had to endure the horrible grinding and scrapings that marked the start of our journey as the rust began to be loosened. Attempting to move after not doing so for a significant time is trying enough, and it only worsens when you are toting thousands of pounds of worthless cargo behind you. Nevertheless, as the Engineer continued to heap coal into my chamber, I felt the cars' weight lessen. As my furnace now roared in flame, it began to purify my insides of the rust of time thus allowing me a freer range of movement. The process was a slow one which required the Engineer's constant attention.

The work, which was toilsome for us both, nevertheless was a spectacle to behold. The creaking and squealing sounds which had started off soon after I began to move now died away as the rust around my wheels fell away—stripped as it were—of its power to arrest. Small bits of coal refusing to burn up in my furnace shot out through my smokestack to become like great crackling fireworks in the sky. Soon, the smoke no longer billowed out as thickly, for the ashes settled in my furnace had been burned away. Instead, a lighter smoke that smelled sweet puffed gently out, the by-product of the Engineer's blazing coal. The Engineer beamed with joy at the sight of this and pulled the whistle in my cabin which sounded out low and fierce like the roar of a lion. It filled my heart with courage as I raced down the tracks, picking up speed. So fast was I travelling now that the wind began to chip away at my black and dusty paint. I winced in pain but was comforted by the Engineer who beckoned me ever forward with a booming voice and the roaring of the lion's whistle. As he did, the chipping of my paint revealed, beneath, another coat which shone like the sun. I scarcely could believe my eyes for I had no memory of ever receiving *this* paint!

How long have I been sitting there, I wondered, *that I even forgot what I looked like*?

Turning my eyes forward, I looked down the track to see an arched bridge appear, which connected the tracks across the vastness of a great canyon. As I grew near, I realized, with no small amount of concern, the track did not connect all the way across and the canyon's middle was a gaping chasm out of which spat molten lava from the deep! If I continued along this way, I felt sure I would speed off the tracks and become a smoking wreckage, one that is all twisted up for people to look upon with the same eerie curiosity they would an old plane wreck stuck on the remote part of a mountain. The very idea of this caused my heart to sink and I began to question the sanity of the one directing me. What sort of route was I being taken on that led to such an impassable blockage?

Then, my concern multiplied tenfold as I saw the lava take an almost sentient shape. It grew into a spectral figure with tigerlike jaws and the eyes of a shark that has been without food for days. Terror began to grip my heart and I called out to the Engineer, though *he* did not think to brake. Instead, he reached quickly for the lever in my cabin which controlled our speed and shifted it forward so that it was set at its maximum. Then he took a mighty breath and blew into my furnace, causing the flames to burn even hotter so that I sped even faster toward that horrid hole in the earth and the flaming beast that now bared its teeth. My heart began to swell as I stared headlong into my greatest fear, chiefly that I would fall into those clamping teeth of burning flame and be melted inside out and twisted into some horrible, unrecognizable shape that would crash and clatter as it fell into a deepening abyss so bright with rage that all before me would be blind to my crushed eyes. I opened my own mouth with all my might to protest to the Engineer. However, I was drowned out by the roaring of the lion as the Engineer now kept the whistle blowing—anchored down with his strong right hand. Staring at the molten earth that leapt out from the chasm, I saw its jaws open to consume me and instinct forced me to shut my eyes and brace for whatever pain came next.

But then the most curious thing happened; I heard the soft padding of feet beside me. As I reopened my eyes, I saw the image of a lion with a mane of golden flame dashing beside me on the tracks. His eyes glinted with a dangerous love as he surpassed me and pounced into the jaws of flame, with his mighty claws outstretched, beating down the beast! The lava twisted itself and fell under the weight of the great golden cat, and so the flames receded with the lion down into the chasm. Then came the moment when we ran out of track and I expected to follow the two creatures to my own doom. Unexpectedly, however; when I passed over the chasm, my wheels departed from the tracks and my whole frame began soaring through the air. The smoke that billowed from my stack had thickened from the Engineer's breath and wrapped itself all about my cabin and coal car so that I was carried above the chasm unharmed! Then I suddenly felt a sharp pain and heard a great snapping of metal which caused me to look backwards. To my utter shock and amazement, I saw that the coupling between my coal car and the rest of my train had torn from the upward strain, sending my trailing burdens headfirst into the fire where they were consumed by the battle of the lion and the flames.

The Engineer cheered when he saw this, his eyes wet with tears. And I in turn began to cry as well—thick droplets which watered the face of my frame. With his dusty handkerchief, the Engineer reached out to my face and gently dabbed up all my tears. He then reached again for the lever that controlled my speed and shifted it so that we slowed down and gently landed where the tracks continued on the other side. As my load was far lighter now, he no longer shoveled in as much coal. Even so, he did not cease entirely, keeping a watchful eye on my hearth to make sure the flames were maintained. Without the train behind us, I found our journey both quicker and smoother. Soon, I watched with joy as the canyon and the bridge began to recede behind us, gradually disappearing into the horizon line.

2

In the Heart of the Forest

I SOON DISCOVERED WE were now traveling through a green field that was alive with all sorts of flowers and grasses. Bees and butterflies and all sorts of tiny creatures jumped around their stalks and drank sweet nectar that dripped down the flowers' petals. Numerous birds could be seen landing and taking off from various patches of the field. As I rode past them, they looked to me and chirped their approval of my shiny frame.

"What a beautiful steam engine!" they called out. "Its countenance is well maintained by its Engineer. Look how he beams from inside the engine's cab! Locomotive, you are loved! You are loved! You are loved!"

"Why, thank you!" replied the Engineer jovially. "I do care greatly for this engine!"

He doffed his cap to the birds in thanks before increasing my speed again and bidding the meadow farewell with two short pulls of the roaring whistle. Shortly thereafter, we began to journey through a forest which had stood on the edge of the vast meadow. The iron tracks on which we rode were covered in moss and lichen and I felt their softness under my wheels as we passed slowly through the trees. Life flowed through the forest so that every which way I looked, I saw green things. Many creatures, big and small, went about the forest floor and skittered through the network of branches that ran overhead and beside the railroad. Unlike the birds I had seen in the meadow, the creatures of the forest did not call out to me. Instead, they passed by me with nervous glances on their faces, for woods can be fearful places, providing many spots for dark and evil things to hide.

The deeper into the forest we went, the less the sun's rays shone through the branches. Eventually, the Engineer flipped a switch to turn on my headlights. At first the connection was weak, and my lights were dim. The Engineer removed his gloves and began to do fine work with my wiring so the connection was strengthened, and my headlamp cut through the ever-thickening shadows like a blade of light. Though I was afraid of the dark, I kept my eyes forward and my ears attuned to the Engineer's voice, allowing his words to encourage my frightened soul. Eventually, we came to the heart of the forest and therein was the darkness and I could not see the tracks except where the light shone. A great creaking sound began to penetrate my thoughts. At first, I heard it as the stretching and compressing of live wood—perhaps the elder elm trees I saw lining the sides of the tracks. But there was no wind present in the forest's heart. As I listened closer, the sound evolved into a metallic cacophony of twisting metals. It caused my mind to spin, and the longer I listened the queasier I became. I at once shut my eyes, opening them again only to find the heart of the forest groaning more horridly as we passed.

"Your light is painful to the forest's heart," the Engineer said with a hint of sadness in his voice. "It has been in the dark for so long the light is unfamiliar to it. It is now filled with fear and pain at seeing this new and drastic change."

"That is most sad!" I said, crying out to the Engineer. I began thinking of how my own heart had once been filled with darkness, a coffin full of ash and dust. But once the light entered, oh how I longed for it to fill me up!

"Surely there is something we can do for this forest!" I said with a quavering voice.

"We already are," the Engineer knowingly replied, "Look at how the forest becomes accustomed to your lamp!"

And as I looked around once more, I noticed how the trees began to shake less as their eyes became familiar with the light of the train lamp. Their branches, which were black as night, had begun to react to the lucent beams that shot forth from my frame like golden daggers. At first, they felt its sharpness cutting through their hardwood shells like the pricking of needles. The longer we were present around the trees, however, their bark began to soften so that the light no longer hurt as it hit them. The old leaves they carried on their gnarled branches now began to fall off, replaced by little green buds. I soon had the urge to stop so my light could continue to feed the forest's heart, but the Engineer did not reach for my brakes. Puzzled, I asked him why he did not stop. The corner of his mouth turned upward in delight as he heard my request.

"Don't worry, friend!" he said with a grin. "We won't leave the forest's heart to linger in the darkness."

The Engineer then reached into a box that was inside the cabin of my frame and pulled out a glass lamp. Taking out a long white candle, he held its wick toward the open hearth. The flames were now roaring with desire for the healing of this place, and out of the dancing fire, a single flame outstretched a burning limb to light the candle's tip. I was surprised to see it glow a bright white instead of the golden yellow of my hearth flames. Before I could query the Engineer for an answer, however, he placed the lit candle in the glass lamp, shut its door and tossed it out my window where it went flying toward the heart of the forest.

In an instant, one of the elder trees reached out with a long arm to break the flying container with a whip-like crack. The glass shattered sending the candle falling to the cold, damp loam that lined the floor of the forest's heart. I began to fear the light would go out as it fell into a pile of wet, decaying mulch; but, to my amazement the floor immediately caught flame! White fire from the candle's wick raced across the damp ground, causing moisture to evaporate and tendrils of hot steam to reach out of the soil toward the upper canopy. As the heat rose, it broke through the thick shroud of the elder trees and brought the sunlight to bear in the heart of the forest. The trees began to shriek at first as the sun revealed the nature of their gnarled, twisted bark, but soon the white flames made their way to the trees themselves, burning off all their impurities so that they fell to the ground with loud thuds. Each nob and growth that fell burned as a fire of its own, at first white—so the fire could spread to the rest of the forest. I soon watched the color of the spreading fire turn to a lively blue which shrank the hideous nobs until they were no larger than pebbles. Then, in a final display of changing color, little flashing red flames burst forth around the leftover impurities consuming them entirely.

Now that the canopy was open to the sun, each green bud was allowed to grow into a leaf so the trees could feed off the warm rays that blanketed the whole of the forest. Wind entered the forest again, running through the branches so the forest swayed and was able to experience the mighty breath of the heavens. At the sight of this, the Engineer began to sing. His voice, ringing with gladness, filled the heart of the forest with delight as he sang of its beauty and its worth.

"How lovely are your leaves, so beautiful and bright!
An elaborate display, of glory and of light!

For you were not left to dwell, forever in the dark.
Feel again the loving kiss of sun upon your bark!

Look how all the creatures, revel in your gaze
And stare upon your newness, offering their praise!

With eagerness they hunger, and beckon to take part
If only just to sing, of the redemption of thy heart!"

As he sang, the Engineer's words came true. Soon, inhabitants of the forest emerged into the light, no longer displaying their previous skittishness.

Raccoons, squirrels, and jays danced among the green leaves laughing with childlike delight. Deer and elk could be seen weaving through the new trees, stopping at each one for a moment to compliment its new complexion before prancing to the next. Several foxes could be seen rolling around on the fresh grass that now sprouted from the forest floor, enjoying the soft feeling on their bright red coats. Even bears could be seen slowly walking through the forest, taking in their new environment with breathless wonder. All the creatures were so distracted by the transformation of the forest heart that they forgot their fear of one another, for their hunger for the light was *far greater* than their hunger for food.

We then began to near the end of the forest. With a sigh of contentment, I turned my gaze once again toward what lay ahead of me on the long iron tracks. Even as we left the forest behind, for many miles I still could hear the creatures of the forest singing and laughing with delight. For though we had left, the heart of the forest was forever changed.

3

Judgment, Justice, and a Vision

Our path eventually took us winding through a series of dry and dusty hills. Some we went over, some under, and some around entirely. A few trees were scattered here and there standing as lone beacons of life in an otherwise desolate area. In this new place, the grass was not green, but yellow and dry on account of being scorched by the sun. No sooner I had observed this then I felt the merciless beating of the sun and began to long for the shade of the forest. I peered searchingly at those few trees present, hoping one or two might offer some respite from the heat, but found myself in a luckless endeavor. Here, the trees were short and wide, unlike the forest where they had grown tall and lean. Although the branches of the hill trees stretched outwards, away from their trunks which were thick and well-rounded, they produced few leaves and in general refused to grow near the tracks. As we passed them by, I called out to them, but received no reply. I then began to wonder if all trees were sentient. Those in the forest obviously had been. After all, regular trees don't have the ability to crack a lantern.

Just as I was opening my mouth to try once more however, another voice called out to me which wasn't the Engineer's. To my surprise, it was the yellow grass I thought was dead that heard my voice.

"Do not trouble yourself with the trees that live in the hills," it said in dry, raspy voice. "They have been asleep for many years and likely will not wake for many more."

Noting sadness in the voice of the grass, I made it a point to inquire more as I went by. "*Why* are they asleep, grass?"

"They haven't had a good drink of water in a long time." The grass sighed. "Sleeping like this is how they conserve their energy."

"And what of you?" I asked this living blanket of the hills. "You seem as though you could use a long drink."

"Oh, indeed!" the grass answered. "I have made it this far by lapping up the morning dew. However, the sun no longer allows me even this. The trees should be fine for a while longer as their roots go deep enough to tap the aquifer, but even this source is running dry."

"How sad," I replied as we began to pull away. "Perhaps we can help!" I beamed, turning to the Engineer. But he did not meet me with a smile this time.

"This area is not yet ready for healing," he said. "So long as those that are alive here remain sleeping, the rains will not come, and this area will turn into a desert."

"But what of this poor grass?" I asked somberly. "Is their life alone not worth saving?"

"Of course!" the Engineer replied in a serious tone. "That grass is more durable than they believe. Even when the sun shrivels up their leaves, still their roots will remain. And when the soil turns to sand, a great wind will sweep down from the mountains and uproot the grass and carry its seeds to a new place."

"Why must it be this way!" I cried out in sadness. "Why must there be so much pain?"

"Healing takes time, my friend." The Engineer spoke with a somewhat sad tone. "Life is *precious*. In some ways the creatures of the earth are very strong. They endure the most excruciating things: the blazing and unforgiving sun, the howling of the winter winds, the freezing rain that stings the skin. All of creation cries out in dismay at how painful life can be, but they endure through these things, nevertheless."

"Then why not heal them *now*? I have seen your power, you healed the forest with your fire!" I asked now, slipping deeper into my feelings of hopelessness.

The Engineer then shifted my speed to its lowest setting, so I continued to pull forward on the tracks at a gentle glide. Climbing out of the cabin, he walked out onto the observation deck that was built on the front of my engine so he could face me. As he looked at me, I noticed tears in his eyes. He reached out a hand and touched my face and I felt his pain. I heard in resolute clarity the crying out of the earth; its pain and sorrow were overwhelming. He removed his hand and the pain began to subside, though I still heard echoes of it ringing in my ears. Then he reached out again and with a single finger touched my chest and I felt an overwhelming sense of love. I suddenly closed my eyes and saw a mighty wave rushing toward me. It towered over everything in sight—even covering up the sun. With my ears, I heard the roaring of the water as it was propelled toward me by the rushing of the wind. It began to arch over me and then it crashed upon me, overtaking me.

But I was not afraid, nor did I feel trapped in that moment. For the glory of the Engineer's love was so great it comforted me as I was swept away by the waters and the winds and the mighty vortex that held me in its grasp. Indeed, I was swept off my feet entirely. The waves took me away from the surety of the earth and out into the great unknown where the waters and the Spirit of creation collide like the ocean crashing on the shore. There I witnessed with awe and wonder how creativity and love mixed together in a beautiful intertwining of the old and the new. For though creation is new, love is older than time itself. And I watched as the Spirit was inspired by the love it experienced so wherever it sent its winds over the earth they rang out like trumpets, announcing the heart of the Creator.

Then, looking above, I saw the Creator *himself* overseeing the workings of the Spirit. He wore robes of white and his eyes shone like fire. As he spoke, the Spirit moved with haste. Then, I looked to his left and I saw a Judge seated on a high and lofty chair with a gavel in his hand. His robes were made of fire and his eyes had a consuming look about them that made me uncomfortable for the first time since I began to witness these things. The Judge sat next to the Creator and spoke words of power over the earth which aligned with the will of the one who was making all things before my eyes. As I looked to the Creator's right, I then saw the Engineer, giddy with excitement at all the Creator did. At each word the Creator spoke, the Engineer would sing out an addition to the Creator's command so that the two were participating with one another in the forming of the world. Then with his two hands, the Creator picked up the Judge and the Engineer and brought them together so that they were one. Unified, they began to survey the farthest reaches of the universe. The keen and fervent eyes of the Judge sought out the darkness in all living things. Anytime he found it, he began to speak judgment over it.

"This is not you. This is not you. This is not you," the Judge said over and over again. I watched as the darkness began to squirm and roil under the weight of his words. As he persisted, it began to leave each creature, whose heart it tightly held like a cancerous growth. As the sickness exited, the creatures would cry out, for parts of each heart were removed with the darkness and they were left with holes unfilled. Then, I witnessed the Engineer sing with his equally bright and merciful gaze into the empty space with the same clear voice he had in the heart of the forest. Then, I watched as each heart began to grow anew. But to my surprise, the words of the Judge changed! He now spoke with a smile as he looked at the restored hearts and said, "This is you. This is you. This is you."

It was in that moment I found myself pulled out of my imagination and back to the iron tracks where the Engineer still stood, looking deep into *my* heart.

"I understand," I said softly. "Your heart for creation is so much greater than I had imagined."

"I will leave *nothing* to the darkness," he said. "I will not leave a single seed, pebble, or grain of sand untouched by the healing I am bringing over the Earth." After he spoke these words, he climbed back into the cabin and increased my speed again.

4

A New, Familiar Place

As we weaved through the hills, I began to wonder where he would take me next. I had come so far and seen so much that I could not imagine what else lay before me. But still we continued as the track lay out beyond my sight. A while after I had pondered this, we crested a hill which revealed a long and deep valley of the most verdant green. Usually such a valley would have a sustaining river or stream running along its floor, but as I began my usual observations, I noted this one contained no such feature. I found this odd, of course, and began searching as we descended for the source of what was keeping this place so lush.

As we started our traverse, I observed countless fruits on the vine, ripe and ready for picking. But where was the water source? I still could not see what fed these plants and kept them from drying out. The sun was still high in the sky and there was not a cloud to be seen. Even so, it wasn't hot in the valley and the closer to the floor we found ourselves, the cooler it became. We soon started our approach on a wide grove of trees and again, as I had not experienced since the start of our journey, I felt the wind on my frame. I watched as it pressed soothingly through the branches of each tree. The valley trees readily submitted themselves to the pulling of the wind as it wove through their forms and caused them to sway. As they swayed, they sang in the most soft and gentle voices I had ever heard. I strained my ears to hear the words but realized, however they were singing, it was not with any audible voice. The farther we descended, the clearer the song became in my mind. It seemed to rise up from the ground itself, much like the green vines that characterized this area, arranging into a harmonic symphony that stirred my heart. I became so distracted by this wonderous sound that I did not see a structure appear beside the tracks.

There stood a tower in the middle of this valley with a pipe that ran down its side and a spout that stuck outwards and hung over the tracks. The Engineer slowed my speed and we came to a stop, directly next to the tower. It was then, as I breathed in, I began to smell fresh water and I realized I was thirsty. *Perhaps this is the source of the water,* I began to think to myself. The Engineer whistled cheerily as he stepped out of my cabin and walked over to the tower. He then moved out of sight for a few minutes and then reappeared with several attendants who looked very much like the firemen I had seen in the beginning. They talked eagerly to the Engineer, asking him how they could be of assistance. He then gestured toward my boiler and they laughed with excitement and nodded in agreement.

There were four of them, each young and bright in appearance. They bore characteristics of the Engineer and worked with such efficiency I concluded they must have done this many times before. One attendant went to open my boiler, which was now quite low on water. I had journeyed many miles without refilling so it was certainly time for a refill. Another attendant brought out a hose which he connected to the spout of the water tower. The other two worked various valves and pumps until fresh water began to pour out of the hose and into my boiler. The water was cold and refreshing, its sweet taste somehow reminded me of the fragrance of flowers most familiar to me. But, as I tried to envision what they looked like, I could not form a single image in my mind or remember even where it was I had seen them. As the cool water made contact with the hot steel of my boiler's shell, a loud hissing sound was generated. Long fingerlike streams of evaporated water danced off of the sides of the boiler and intertwined with one another to form a mystical swirling cloud that was both thrilling to look at and yet oddly reminiscent of a previous experience. The more I observed about this place, the more I began to feel I had somehow been here before. Each tree now seemed to me like some friend I had grown up with. Each shrub, a neighbor most dear for whom I had cared. For a moment, I forgot all about my quest to find the valley's water source and I turned to the Engineer to ask for clarity on another matter.

"My dearest friend," I began quietly, "I cannot shake the feeling I have been here before. Tell me, if you know, when and how it was I came to this wonderful place. If it is true I am from this place, I cannot imagine why I ever left it!"

The Engineer, who had been surveying the attendants in their work, now turned his gentle disposition to rest upon me and began to answer, "Many who visit this valley feel as you do now. There are many reasons for this." He did not elaborate on what those reasons were. Somewhat disappointed with this response, I begged him to continue.

"This is a wonderful place, my friend!" he said with his usual smile. "Here is a valley where the Creator's spirit dwells in the flesh! His presence waters the earth and he does not hide himself from the creatures of this place," he said with a chipper grin. I felt a lightning bolt go off in my brain, with a loud thunderous crash of clarity following it. So *that* was the source. I left that thought to the side for now though and continued my previous line of questioning.

"Then *why* do I feel that I remember this place from long ago?" I asked.

"You feel this is familiar, because we all long to dwell in the presence of the Creator. It is what all creatures are made for."

It was only for a moment, but something in his words pulled me briefly back to reality. I remembered who I was and all the purpose that had led me right to the day when the engineer had found me. But, like the tendrils of steam that had begun to clear as my refilled boiler was latched back to a close, the memory of my true self dissipated and retreated back to the recesses of my mind.

I wanted to ask the Engineer more, but before I had the chance he turned away and thanked the attendants for their aid. He then hopped back into the cabin of my engine where he released my brakes and I began to chug forward once again on the long iron tracks. As I passed by, the attendants cheered and wished me the best on my journey. I thanked them with my words and then it occurred to me that I should perhaps blow my whistle to show my gratitude. The Engineer was more than happy to comply, and the valley was soon echoing with the powerful roars of the lion who continued to beckon me forward on my journey.

5

The Sea and the Storm

Our exit from the valley brought us to bear upon a plain where tall grasses swayed in the wind. Like the trees in the valley, they too sang out a most melodious sound and I was encouraged. It was then the Engineer called to my attention what was coming into focus on the horizon. There, perhaps several miles down the track, *I saw the sea*. A vast blue and gray line now appeared and I began to watch it grow ever larger as we made our approach. The wind grew stronger the closer we came so that I felt a strong force pushing against me as I moved down the line.

The approaching sea filled my mind with an array of questions. Were the tracks to take me across? How many trains had taken this path before me? My mind tossed and rolled in sync with the billowing white crests of the sea's waves which crashed upon the craggy shores—a fortress wall built to keep the ocean from flooding the interior. We then came to the place where the tracks departed from the land and continued on over the vastness of the waters. They were kept above the ocean by a long and rocky jetty which the waves persistently pressed against from both sides.

As I peered forward, I could see no end. The tracks continued far out beyond the horizon where, as near as I could tell, they did not stop for a substantial distance. Then, the farther I looked I noticed something which filled me with trepidation. A pillar of black clouds taking the shape of a blacksmith's anvil sat wrathfully over the iron tracks. This was the storm. My heart beat faster.

Surely the Engineer did not mean to take me by this route, I thought with horror. No sooner had those words crossed my mind than a troupe of grey gulls flew up beside my engine and shouted a warning in my ears, "Turn back, engine! The way is not safe! Before you lies a mighty storm whose anger is great. He means to crush the way across the seas and drown anyone who attempts to cross!"

These cautionary words were reinforced in my mind as I heard the ravings of the storm. With his arms he reached into the firmament and pulled down ice and snow to add to his volatile collection of twisting elements. As he did this, he shouted out his displeasure for the tracks and the jetty that held them up. With the force of his stinging wind, he called upon the ocean to aid him in his efforts to drown the tracks and bury them beneath the seas. The same waves I had seen lashing out at the craggy beach could now be seen beating against the rocks that held up the tracks. Each violent crash sent up ocean spray that fell on the tracks so that the rocks and the iron and the wooden ties were all damp. I then turned my eyes back toward the dark swirling mass shouting words of fear every which way he could. Lightning shot out from his body at various angles and struck the surface of the sea causing large smoke clouds to cover the waters, impeding my vision of the tracks. It was at this point I was now within view of the storm. Two eyes of emerald green appeared from within the swirling and I understood he was looking at me. He spoke with anger as his voice thundered out across the open ocean.

"How *dare* you approach me!" he said. "Flee now from this place for you cannot pass!"

The Engineer did not allow me the opportunity to reply as he increased my speed to its maximum once again. My heart beat wildly in trepidation as we sped out across the seas. I wanted to stop at this point and tried desperately to communicate this to my pilot, but the Engineer did not break, even for a moment. Instead, he began to hum a deep tune from his powerful lungs. Words began to appear in my mind that spoke to me of courage and strength.

"I am with you. I am with you. I am with you," they said.

I was so afraid my voice froze up and I could not speak. It was as I felt the fear welling up inside of me, however, I noticed the Engineer now standing once again on the observation deck—staring defiantly into the heart of the storm.

This angered the storm more than anything, so he began to collect his energy together and strike us in his fury. I shut my eyes and braced for impact, expecting to be crushed by the force of his strike when once again the lion's roar resounded.

When I opened my eyes, the Engineer was nowhere to be found. Instead, I saw the golden lion who had batted down the jaws of flame earlier in my journey. He ran out in front of me and jumped into the heart of the storm where he was kept out of sight behind a wall of hail, rain, and lighting strikes. I heard the storm howling in pain as he battled the lion. The lion's roars not only echoed out across the seas, but emitted flashes of light that allowed me to view snap shots of the battle. The lion leapt into the sky undeterred by the ice shards that pelted his shimmering coat of gold. His claws lashed at the darkness, creating tears of light within the twirling and twisting of the storm. With each cut he received, the Storm's power dwindled so that he grew tired and began to breathe heavily. It was at this point I, still rushing forward on the tracks, pushed through the wall of the storm and into the eye where I could now see the ensuing battle.

But I no longer saw the lion.

Instead, I saw a small and gentle lamb licking the wounds of the storm, comforting him in his pain! The storm wailed in agony but was gradually calmed by the power of the lamb so the winds began to die down and the seas calmed as a result. And when the storm finally stopped lashing out, the lamb began to sing in a voice most sweet so that the storm was lulled to sleep, and the clouds broke, allowing the sun to shine upon the heart of the storm.

In utter amazement, I watched as the light revealed the form of an elderly man with many wrinkles on his brow. I saw in his body a frailness I had not seen before. He appeared exhausted from many years of work, and on his hands were numerous scars and callouses. Then I watched as the lamb transformed before my eyes into the golden lion from before and began carrying the old man on his back, still asleep, with the man's face gently resting on the lion's soft fur. From my angle, I saw the back of the man, which was laid bare and open due to tears in his shirt which he had made as he was flailing about. On it were long lashes and his flesh was black and blue from beatings he had received.

At first, I thought perhaps it was the lion that had delivered such blows to him, but then I saw in the clouds yet another vision. I saw first a young man, spry and full of energy, toiling in a long field. Then suddenly, a group of men with the most wicked of expressions came upon the worker and began to beat him with their fists. As the worker fell, the men kicked him with their boots until he lay prostrate on the ground, unable to defend himself. They tore his shirt and began to whip him ferociously with a nine-tailed whip that had barbs and shells and other sharp objects sewn into the hard leather straps hanging from its boney handle. With each strike, his flesh was torn open so he was left in agonizing and unspeakable pain. It was then revealed to me this was the same man I saw on the back of the lion. For years he had received such treatment until he was eventually driven to despair, his spirit becoming enraged like a storm.

I was amazed, because what I had interpreted as a battle between the lion and a storm most vile was actually an act of mercy whereby the lion and the lamb met creation in the midst of its pain and fought *with* it to bring about a reconciliation. I watched with joy as the lion climbed into the sky where the heavens opened up to receive him and the elderly man the lion bore. A host of radiant beings were waiting on the edges of heaven with arms outstretched to pull up the man's limp body. And as he was carried into the realm of the Creator, his age faded away until I saw the younger version once again.

Therein was his life, full and without anguish. For the storm inside his soul had now dissipated and given way to the tender flesh of a living, breathing man. I watched him awaken with joy to his surroundings, his eyes full of tears.

"I thought I was lost forever," he said.

And at this, the lion roared his most ferocious battle roar, for he was angered by the man's words. Not at the one who spoke them, but because the lion knew how much pain had been caused by the man's misplaced belief in them.

6

How I Came to Know

THEN IT WAS THAT the Engineer appeared once more in my cabin and I was brought back to my location on the long iron tracks. My mind swam with marvel at the images I had seen. Not only had I witnessed battle, but the binding up of wounds. I had seen judgment, but also restoration. I had seen a grace most life-giving, but also ferocious. For it was the claws of the lion that had ripped through the storm wall and allowed the sun to shine into the heart of the storm. The dissipation of the clouds now allowed me a wide range of unimpeded vison so I could see for many miles in all directions.

The surface of the seas was no longer choppy, but rather smooth and glassy so that as I rode forward on the jetty I could clearly see my reflection in the waters. My golden color shown out distinctly as the sun's rays reflected across my metallic frame. I felt the wind again on my face, but it was no longer cold or harsh as before, but soft and warm, reminiscent of the lush green valley. Fish jumped out of the water for the first time as I flew by on the tracks, thanking the Engineer for clearing the storm. He replied to them in much the same way as I had now seen him do on multiple occasions.

It now occurred to me there was some pattern to our journey I had not noticed until this moment. It seemed to me less and less that this journey was about me, but about the places which the Engineer took me to. Some places were pleasant and full of color, and so I was filled with delight. Meanwhile, others I found to be empty or full of pain, and so I felt sorrow. When would the journey end? How many places would I be led to see? The Engineer seemed to read my thoughts as he spoke to me from inside the cabin of my engine.

"All journeys have an end. No one was made to wander forever."

"But when and how will it end? My mind is swirling with a desire to *know*," I confessed timidly.

The Engineer paused for a moment in thought and then spoke clearly to my question, saying, "Knowledge is a powerful thing. It can tell us how things are in the past, present, and even sometimes in the future. It comes from a desire to seek the *truth* in the world; to know which course of action is good and upright. Therefore, your desire to know is not inherently bad."

"Then *why* not tell me?" I pleaded.

"Because your thirst for knowledge comes as a result of your searching for an answer to your *fears*," he said with a downcast voice. "Were I to tell you of the end, then you would become so focused on its coming about that you would no longer live in the present."

I sighed softly, as the truth of his words occurred to me, for I had been afraid greatly during each encounter we had with the darkness. Had I known the outcome, I would not have been as excited nor as amazed by what I saw. Instead, I would have feared whether the events themselves were truly the ones that had been spoken to me, because wherever there is knowledge, so too there is doubt.

"Do you remember your name?" the Engineer suddenly asked me, continuing our conversation. But at this intimate and penetrating question, my heart began to beat fast. I searched my memory for that which I was called at the time of my creation; it was on the tip of my tongue now. Even so, I struggled to form the word on my lips and in frustration, I admitted to the Engineer that I could not remember.

"You *know* it," he said to me, as we continued to ride forward. "It has been said to you time and time again. I have even called you by it several times on this journey and yet you struggle to bring it into reality."

"Why then can I not remember?" I wondered aloud.

"Because *knowing* is not the same thing as *believing*." the Engineer said.

At this, I felt a jolt of energy run through me and my name began to appear to me in my mind. I saw it in its totality, every syllable made clear. Even so, I still could not find the strength to say it aloud.

"Do not be afraid!" the Engineer encouraged me.

My heart began to well up inside of me so that my name was pushed out of my lungs, travelling through my throat where it sat on the edge of my tongue. I opened my mouth only for a moment and there it escaped, like a young bird flying from the nest!

"My name is *Courage*!" I burst out. The unexpected force of my name caused it to echo out loudly across the open seas. At this, the Engineer began to clap loudly while cheering with delight.

"*Yes,* it is!" he said with a thunderous voice before pulling the lion whistle. "Where you feel weakest, is actually where you are *strongest*. I go with you into places of fear and darkness because you are Courage, which is a mighty foe to these things."

"How can that be so?" I asked, puzzled.

"Your fellow creatures also need encouragement to believe they are who I have said they are. The forest was afraid it was a place of darkness, and not one of life. Your light became a source of healing for it because you reminded the forest of its true identity!"

"But *you* were the one who lit the forest aflame," I replied.

"That is true," the Engineer said, "But only after the forest asked me to restore it like I did you."

I then realized I had no memory of the forest ever speaking. "I thought the forest didn't want us there."

I spoke, remembering how the trees had lashed out at the Engineer's lantern, breaking it before it could even land on the ground. Then the Engineer amazed me with what he spoke next.

"It was not out of fear that the trees broke the lantern, but out of an eagerness to be renewed."

"Oh, how wonderful! My heart is overflowing!" I shouted. "There is no end to your love," Said I to the Engineer, with teary eyes.

"Indeed," said the Engineer with a content smile. "There is no end."

7

The Aftermath, Afterthoughts, and Afterward

As we continued to race down the tracks across the seas, I thought more on what the Engineer had told me; of my name—Courage—and of the vastness of his renewing love for the creatures of the Earth, even the ones that seemed violently unapproachable. *How strange was this form of love,* I thought, *that it so quietly crept up on me*? For there never was a moment when the Engineer shouted at me to pick myself up, dust out my insides, and journey onward, alone. Instead, he approached me with such gentle grace that one should think I was his toddler rather than an engine made of iron and steel.

As we passed over the last few miles of the jetty, I began to see in the distance the next location of our journey. There, towering over a white beach and a meadow of soft green grass was a mountain higher than any I had ever seen. Its base was thick and strong, such that I could tell even from a fair distance that its roots reached deep into the earth. Many evergreens picketed the sides of the great monolith, tapping into its abundant nutrients and underwater reservoirs. So high did it reach, I could not see its crown above the puffy white clouds that settled themselves comfortably around its form.

"That is Mt. Elon!" said the Engineer pointing with excitement. "He is the tallest mountain on earth and a great friend to creation! For many eons he has stood watch over creation, a high tower of protection. We go now to climb his peak."

A playful wind jostled us as we left the jetty and began to race toward Elon's base. I saw here on the other side of the sea a great many new things. The trees, which smiled at me as I passed by, were of some foreign variety I had not known existed. Looking out into the meadow, I saw what I thought appeared to be sheep, though they too were obviously native to this land and no other. A sweet smell seemed to persist here, an indication the land was abundant with fruits to be eaten and enjoyed. Much like the valley of rest I had gone through, this place filled me with an eagerness to stay and enjoy my surroundings. I soon began to picture myself at the next stop where I might enjoy a fresh rest and absorb with eyes and ears the fullness of the flora and fauna of this paradise. I took a deep breath and readied myself for the Engineer's inevitable break, but such a moment did not come. Instead, we continued to race toward Elon and the long shadow which he cast over the land like a comforting grey blanket. All the while, we passed bright flowers and strong trees that stood tall, the likes of which I found intriguing and entirely unfamiliar.

I began to be discouraged for I wished to stay and meet them. I felt anxiety welling up within me at every perceived lost opportunity to relish the beauty of the Creator whom I had come to admire so greatly. The Engineer, it seemed, was totally oblivious to my growing discomfort as he kept his eyes fixed solely on the mountain. I wanted to reach out and grab the sides of the tracks with iron claws and forcibly slow myself down. I wanted to dig my fingers and toes into the fertile ground and press back against the forward motion dictated by the Engineer. But I could not bring myself to voice these thoughts, as I was ever so timid in the bringing of them to life. Instead, I let them collect and clutter up my insides like a large pile of wet leaves under an oak tree in the deep of winter. Indeed, I felt the same slimy consistency one might feel if they came across such a pile, strewn about on the fresh loam, collecting and decaying. A simple prod with a broken branch would reveal beneath, the insects and forest bugs that hide in those darkened and damp conditions. In my heart, those insects took the names of Doubt, Uncertainty, and Fear. I felt each one scurry about, collecting a little material here and nibbling a bit of crinkled leaf there. As they did so, they threatened to grow and multiply, because one small bit of doubt or fear or uncertainty can easily multiply. It is the nature of such things that live in the darkness. Without the gardener or groundskeeper to come along and rake up the leaves, we would find the warm greenery of our hearts replaced by a depressive layer of cold earth.

I then realized how uncomfortable I had become, and incidentally I noticed I had begun to slow down. My first thought was the Engineer had finally taken notice of my falling spirits and was adjusting our itinerary to match. But this, it seemed, was not the case, for as I turned my gaze back down the long iron tracks, I noticed a fork. Two paths were stretched out before me, both seeming to lead toward the peak of Mt. Elon. We stopped briefly so the Engineer could operate a switch beside the track, thereby directing our route toward the right rather than the left. Wordless as he worked, the Engineer did not address my unstable state, though I was sure my anxiety must have been noticeable to him by now. Once he was finished, and our course set, the Engineer hopped back into the cab and we veered to the right and began ascending the base of Mt. Elon.

Here at the bottom, I was given an excellent vantage point of Elon's magnitude. From a distance, he had appeared to be large, but I was shocked to find he was far larger than I had expected. As I looked up in awe to where the clouds shrouded Elon's crown, I noticed several eagles flying just below. Suddenly, one of the eagles pumped its mighty wings and ascended into the white layer of nimbus that hide Elon's mount from the ground where it then disappeared out of sight. A few moments later, I watched another eagle do the same, and eventually (as I spent several minutes observing) I witnessed a handful of eagles, different from those I had seen entering, descend through the cloud bank. The whole display was so intricate and intentional that for a moment I forgot my disappointment and submitted an observation to my guide.

"I find it curious," I wondered aloud, "that so many eagles are gathered at Elon's peak."

"They are messengers," the Engineer told me with delight. "They visit Elon to hear the will of the Creator, for the mountain serves as the meeting place of the heavens and the Earth."

"What do they do with the Creator's words once they have received them?" I asked.

"Why, they take them with care back to their people of course!" the Engineer replied enthusiastically. I began to think of this relationship between the eagles and the Creator and many questions thus appeared within me that I was eager to ask the Engineer. This time, however, he noticed my inner disposition and calmly reassured me each question I had would be answered soon.

"We are going to the top," he said pointing toward the clouds. "There, you will have the chance to ask the Creator yourself!"

At these words, my heart began to soar! How long had I waited to meet the Creator! Oh, how many questions I had! There were so many I could have written several books with the answers the Creator might give. My mind rattled around trying to keep them intact and I began to sort out which I might ask first (as I assumed the Creator of the universe to be very busy) followed by those I might ask later if time permitted. In the joy of these thoughts, my doubts were subjugated and eclipsed. As my mind became transfixed on the glory I might see, my heart forgot all about my fear of the passage of time, and all the good things I had missed fully enjoying. The reader might find this reality strange of course, but anyone who has even caught a glimpse of the thing they desire the most will know exactly what I am referring to. Even good things pale in comparison with that which is *greatest*.

8

The Silver Engine

It was at this point on the journey, as I rode along dreaming of better things, that the long iron tracks began to slope upwards. I then found myself breathing quite heavily, for even though the incline was not especially steep, the effort required to haul my large frame upwards was still substantial. Within minutes, I found my heart growing tried, and my inner doubts beckoning me to return from whence I had come, back down into the green and pleasant valley below. But, before I had the chance to voice such fears, my eyes caught the shape of something I had not yet seen on the journey. *I saw another engine.*

She was smaller than me, with a beautiful coat of silver paint that reflected the exceptional clarity of a summer lake. She too had an attached coal car and I observed, as we approached, her furnace was already lit, and out of her smokestack puffed gently the same sweet smells of the valley below. We began to slow as we approached, and I noticed she did not travel on the same track as I did, but on one that ran beside it. I then gathered that this must be the other way up mount Elon! Whereas I had taken the right route, she had taken the left. As we came gently to a halt beside her, she did not speak out. I heard, instead a quiet whimper and observed a steady stream of tears running down her face. I took this moment of pause in our journey to catch my breath and regather my own strength, as Mt. Elon's peak was still quite a way off. Though, as I did so, I looked over at the silver engine, who was now being looked over by the Engineer. The Engineer displayed a degree of concern as he attempted to console her.

"Why have you stopped here, oh precious one?" he gently asked.

She turned her eyes to meet his and with a soft voice replied, "I am too weak to climb the mountain . . . but neither do I have the courage to turn around and go back either."

At these words, I suddenly felt my heart begin to grow in a manner that dispersed my anxiety and my doubt, those tiny insects fleeing under the sudden casting of light—a ray of sun that emitted from a place deeper than the crevices of my soul—and I called out, "I will go with you! The Engineer and I are making the same journey!"

My words surprised the silver engine, who stopped crying and looked over at me instead. I too was shocked by my own suggestion, which flew out unexpectedly.

"If you like," I continued, "I will run this course alongside you while the Engineer comforts you from within. He has been such an encouragement to me on my journey."

I then looked over to the Engineer, who did not speak but nodded his agreement. A wide smile ran across his face, and I knew he was pleased with my suggestion. The silver engine then turned to face the Engineer and said, "I should like that very much, though I am not sure I will make it to the top."

The Engineer then turned to the both of us and said with a keen look in his eyes, "What a wonder it is, that where such great strength lies in plenty it is barred with faithlessness in equal measure."

Before either I or the silver engine could reply to these strange words however, he hopped into her cabin and once again assumed his role as the Engineer. I watched thereafter as the silver engine grew in strength, summoning a boldness that had simply lay dormant before the Engineer, in his typical fashion, stoked it to life once more.

Soon, we were off again. The journey up Mt. Elon proved to be an arduous climb, which we took at a slow but steady pace. Such strain I had not known before, for with every inch of ground we gained the next proved to be more difficult. The iron tracks creaked and groaned sharply as our wheels bit hard along the rails to secure as strong a grip as we could.

Every now and then, the Engineer would travel back over to my cab to ensure I did not lose the fire in my own hearth. As he did so, I noticed for the first time the Engineer's brow thick with perspiration. For even as our speed up the mountain was quite slow, it proved to be a burdensome task to run alongside the tracks, going between our two engines. But even as he sweat and the strain of heaving coal began to show itself on his sagging shoulders, his spirit did not dim. And I saw burning within his eyes the same dangerous love which had shown brightly from the eyes of the lion that had emerged every time we encountered adversity.

I began to understand more clearly. Images, as sharp as though I were looking out presently with my eyes, quickened themselves to the forefront of my mind. I saw the lion and the engineer walking towards one another, each in a manner both natural to their own form and yet curiously like the other whom they approached. Though the lion padded forward on all fours, there was something regal and upright in its gait. Meanwhile, I observed in the engineer's ambulation an almost animal-like disposition. From underneath the Engineer's cap, I saw a golden mane begin to grow so that he appeared as a prince wearing a fine coat. And as he walked, the motion caused the coat to twist so an array of light cascaded outwards. It did not shoot out in sharp cutting beams but flowed from the hems of the coat like thick honey, burnished by the sun and warm to the touch.

Curious still, I watched the lion's fur become covered in ash and smoke as I had often seen the Engineer. And the burden of time announced its mark under the eyes of the lion, which soon turned grey, resembling cold stones. The lion stumbled and fell into a mist that had only just blown in from some faraway place so that I lost sight of the mighty creature for a moment. But the

Engineer did not stop walking toward the lion, remaining undeterred by the mist. With purposeful strides, he continued to approach the great beast. And with each step he took, I watched as all remnants of the dusty, weathered Engineer gave way to a tall and kingly man. When he was on the edge of the mist, he stopped and cupped his hands together around his lips and with a voice like the mighty crashing of a waterfall spoke out into the dim. As he did, the shroud that had covered the lion disappeared and revealed the shape of a four-legged animal lying on the ground. But as I peered forward, it was not the lion I saw, but the same lamb that had fought against the storm and licked the wounds of the man within.

The king then knelt down and held out his arms, calling the lamb toward him. The lamb stood up, weakly at first with wobbly knees. Its soft coat was as black as soot and clung thickly to the lamb's skin so that it appeared to be covered in oil. But still it managed to make its way over to the open arms of the king who waited patiently with no sign of being irritated or angered. And when the lamb was close, the king took off his cloak and wrapped it around the lamb which caused it to cry out in surprise. The king then picked up the swaddled lamb and began to dry off the blackened oil with his fine coat so its fur once again became as white as snow. And the golden light that surrounded them gave way to blinding white light, so I was unable to perceive through the brilliance, where the king began, and the lamb ended.

9

The Quest, Questions, and What We Saw

SOON THEREAFTER, I WAS once again aware of my surroundings on the long iron tracks. We had now made it about halfway up the mountain. The Engineer had just jumped off the edge of my frame and was now racing back toward the silver engine, huffing and puffing as the Engineer went. I took the moment to once again study the qualities of the silver engine, that I might deduce something about her character. Where had she come from? What was she doing here? Had she been led to Mt. Elon like I had? My desire to know once again welled up within me and a voice from inside called out, *Just ask!*

So I did.

At first, the silver engine was slow to answer my inquiries which intially stumbled out mechanically, but gradually became more natural as we grew accustomed to conversing with one another. All the while, the Engineer listened quietly, focusing mostly on tending to our hearths.

"What drew you to the mountain?" I started out curiously.

After a few moments' pause she said, "It's hard to explain . . . Maybe it was the smell of the flowers or the warmness of the breeze on my face . . . Once I came to this place, I felt myself pulled ever more toward the center, which I assumed to be the mountain."

"And what do you suppose is at the center?" I asked eagerly, though I of course had my own notion of what might be there.

"I have this feeling," she said, searching in her mind for the word that described it. Her brow crinkled as she focused on imagining it. "Like my heart is a magnet and at the center of the mountain is one with the opposite polarity pulling me toward it." She then released herself from the effort of trying to remember and asked the same question to me in return.

"I was not drawn to the mountain," I admitted. "Rather, it seems the mountain was drawn to me."

The silver engine then gave a cheery laugh, which rang out like a sleigh bell from the mountainside. "What do you mean by that?" she queried.

And so I told her my story, how I had sat dormant and rusted on the tracks before the Engineer found me, of the journey we had taken together, and of the many places we had seen along the way. Her eyes lit up as I described the renewing of the forest and the valley of rest that followed. Then, her face darkened as I spoke of the storm which had barred our path. I even recounted to her the visions which had come to me at various times, to which she seemed quite astonished. I then spoke finally of the things which the Engineer had told me regarding the origin of Mt. Elon and the Creator who resided upon its crown whom I was on my way to meet presently.

"I *believe* you will make it to the top and meet this Creator," she said after I had finished.

Unlike her previous words, which she had spoken from a place of reservation, these she announced with a confidence so grounded that my heart began to believe as well. Such power came from the utterance of those simple words that I felt my strength renewing as we pressed onwards toward Elon's crown and the Creator's seat. We had spent so long talking that I hardly noticed the progress we had made. Rounding the wide girth of Elon, we held in our gaze the magnitude of the land of plenty which nestled itself comfortably about the mountain's feet and stretched its long arms out to the sea and in all other directions. As we surveyed the land now far below, it came to us that we now had to pass through the barrier of clouds that had kept Elon's crown hidden from sight.

A sudden gust of wind came galloping from behind us as we clambered through the thick clouds. And with the wind, rounding the corner, came the body of an eagle rising up to pierce the shroud. The eagle's mahogany feathers shimmered as the wind flowed about his wings, propelling him with great speed upwards through the bank. He called out to us as he passed by, beckoning us to move forward and shouting out encouragement as he could before disappearing in the white vapor that now encapsulated us in its soft clasp. The further upwards we traversed, the thicker the cloudbank became until we could no longer perceive each other except by the flickering light exuding from our hearth flames (which could not be diminished by the white shroud that lay now over our eyes).

As I looked about, I saw not one flame other than my own, but *two*. One glowed bright and cheerily like mine, which I knew to belong to the silver engine. But where the Engineer had been walking beside us, there now roared a bright flame of a golden white hue. I watched as it grew warmer and wider until it began to burn off the mist that surrounded us. Soon, the golden flame became so bright it cast a shadow on the ground behind us as we sprinted up the last section of the mountain pathway. I found this to be most curious in that it was like a shadow (casting the image of the one whose form it mimicked) and yet not, for there was no darkness upon the ground. How it is possible to cast a shadow of light, truly I could not say, but in that moment, my eyes did not deceive me. I took comfort in the warmth of the flames and in the light of the sun which had now begun to break through the dissipating mist. And then, I lost my breath.

The passing through of the cloudbank revealed the crown of Elon standing tall and bold, snowless and speckled with oak trees all about. Even at the peak, there was still a substantial amount of land to traverse and I began to take note of the features that defined this land. On Elon's north side rested the summit which, although prominent, contained none of the jagged or forbidding shapes of the mountains I had seen before. Indeed, the mountain was quite smooth, and long grasses could be seen blanketing the crown except for the center and near Elon's summit where the grass was short, as though it had been trimmed. In the center was a lake surrounded by shores of white sand which grew and shrank in size as the waters lapped back and forth in rhythmic motion. The lake was long and bulged at is north end as it faced Elon's summit. I then noticed that a stream fed the lake, trickling down from the open door of a great house that stood built into the side of the mountain peak.

Where the house stood, the grass was cut and carefully maintained, and sectioned by various pathways of smooth marble stones. Pillars wide and tall supported the frame of the great house, which had many levels. I say it was a house because it had eaves and a gabled roof which I thought odd as no snow (or sign of it) could be seen anywhere. Many windows were in the house where sunlight could shine in—or perhaps out, as it was hard to tell whether the constant light that persisted all about was from the sun or some other source.

"It's so beautiful," the silver engine sighed, breaking through my thoughts.

Yes, I thought, not taking my eyes off the beautiful landscape. And then something quite *extraordinary* occurred—I felt the grass between my toes.

10

When We Began to Run

"WHAT!?" I SAID WITH a cry of surprise so loud I startled even myself! I looked down to see that the long iron tracks were gone and in their place were two feet! *My feet.* I reached down to touch them and there I saw hands! *My hands.* I used them to discern the shape of my arms and shoulders working my way eventually up to my face where I then laughed with delight to discover I had eyes, a nose, and two ears! I spun around to face the Engineer and the silver engine but found instead two people I scarcely recognized. The Engineer now appeared kingly, much in appearance like the one I had seen comforting the lamb. All trace of ash and soot was gone from his face and brow, which was now smooth and bright and crowned with wisdom. His clothes had been replaced by fine robes of gold, interlaced with silver bands and dotted with gemstones of a deep blue color. A smile was wide across his face.

Beside him stood a woman I had never seen before. Her face was round and smooth like the Engineer's, and kind and full of life. Her tourmaline eyes shone brightly and seemed to change color as she looked about. Her hair was long and dark and braided down the side of her shoulder, ending at her waist where it was tied off with a silver ribbon. She too was clothed in fine robes, which matched the silver ribbon in her hair and were speckled with many colored gemstones that shimmered as she moved. Her hands were cast into the air like a flower stretching its petals to catch the sun. She laughed aloud, letting the light warm her limbs as her voice rang out like a sleigh bell. It then came to me that this woman was once the silver engine I had traveled with up the mountainside!

"What has happened to us? Why do we appear this way?" I asked, addressing the king.

"Elon's crown has a way of showing things as they truly are," he replied simply, "and it's important you appear so when you go to meet the Creator."

He pointed toward the great house on the far side of the lake which I then understood to belong to the Creator. Excitement began to fill every bone in my new body, and with giddiness I turned about and began to run. As I was barefoot, I felt everything as I ran across the crown, from the springiness of the grass, to the coolness of the rich dirt which provided for the vegetation of this place. I skipped with joy down to the south end of the lake where I finally stopped to breathe again under the shade of a rather wide willow tree, whose long boughs reached out over the water seemingly in an attempt to caress the lake with its drooping leaves (as willows tend to do).

Slowly, I walked up to the edge of the water, that I might catch a glimpse of my new form. In the shade of the willow tree, I was able to find an angle by which the light acted as a mirror on the water and I saw myself for the first time. No trace of my former metallic covering could be seen anywhere about my soft skin. No smoke stack from my head where now came down tufts of sandy hair. My eyes a poignant blue, soft and clear like the waters of the lake. And streaming down my face came such tears of gladness that I smiled brightly at my own reflection, now disrupted by the ripples in the water which resulted from my falling happiness. I too was wearing robes of an orange gold color lined with blue silk that seemed to glow as I moved my arms and legs. It was soft and perfectly fitted to my body, warm under the cool of the willow tree, but light and breathable as I had run across the greenery in the sun. I was soon joined by the Engineer and the woman (whose name I still knew not) who came jogging across the meadow to rest by the waters.

"You are quite the runner!" chirped the woman. "You took off prancing like a deer, it was all we could do to keep up!"

I turned to face her as she stepped gently into the cool waters of the lake beside me.

"What is your name?" I asked eagerly, for I could not go on not knowing any longer. She lifted her eyebrows as her smooth face crinkled once again in a warm laugh.

"I'm sorry I didn't tell you! It had not occurred to me." Then she paused for a moment in thought, looking at the leaves of the willow as the wind blew across the lake, lifting them in its arms.

"My name is Hope," she finally said. "Although I do not know your name either."

"His name is Courage," said the king, stepping beside us into the cool waters. "Something which he often forgets."

Hope then began to stare at me in wonder, and I at her, for names have a way of bringing things to life.

"I see now," she said after a while. "You were brought to help me summit the mountain!"

"Yes," spoke the king directly. "But it was not Courage alone that brought you to the peak. Indeed, Courage would not have made it were it not for Hope."

I knew in my heart that the king's words were true, and I simply nodded my agreement as Hope stared at me in disbelief.

"But I didn't do anything!" she said doubtfully.

"On the contrary," chimed the king, "you did the most important thing of all; you *believed*. Hope is a powerful act that defies the influence of fear. When paired with courage, the *will* to *act* in spite of fear, fear then has little power to impede. That is why you were brought together."

We both stood silent for a moment, taking in the king's words before he spoke again.

"And now it is time to meet the Creator," he said gently. "He has a task for you both to undertake together—if you are willing." In our present state of peace, we could hardly say no, so we both agreed and began to follow the king.

11

The House and its Rooms

The king took us on a pathway that lined the lakeside and wound upwards toward the trimmed grass and the tall house cut into the mountain. The sun was warm on our skin as we walked beside the cool waters, breathing deeply. We did so not because we were denied sufficient oxygen, but rather because we found the air was scented sweetly and most refreshing to inhale. Even so, everything left us breathless. In this way, we found ourselves so surrounded by a wild abundance that no amount of feasting with our searching eyes, listening ears, or trembling skin could leave us satiated. It was as though we held our lips to the passing trail of a cool stream, drinking long but never feeling a need to stop. And thankfully, we were not made to.

I must also point out this state did leave us in *no* place of dissatisfaction. Contradictory though it may seem, the lack of satiation was unlike the low rumbling of a hungry stomach which continues to sound out until the problem has been solved. We hungered instead from our hearts which could not be filled. To be filled would mean we could take on no more, and nothing we experienced left us burdened in any such way, *only eager*. It was with this eagerness we hiked up the marbled steps to the great house on Mt. Elon. As we did so, I noticed for the first time that the house was lacking a key architectural feature: There were no doors. Only a frame stood tall and wide so the wind blew in and out of the house in places other than the windows, all of which were ajar. Other than the lack of closing doors, everything else about the house's structure was normal. Yet, it was the most extraordinary thing I had seen!

Twelve floors, the house contained, and each level was supported by smooth wooden pillars numbering the same. On each pillar was inscribed a song in a unique language, most of which I could not read. And beside each pillar there stood a reader, who sang out the words from the wood which was carved in ornate patterns and buffed so that it shone keenly in the light of the sun's rays. As I listened, I became astounded. For though they all spoke different words, every song seemed to meld together into one harmonious symphony that resounded across the mountain plateau and out into the wide world.

As I looked, I saw the words on the pillars changed and developed with the song so the wood appeared to be in motion, *alive* as it were. And beside each reader, I noticed a writer who stood listening intently. As the song came ringing out, each note and word was recorded on a scroll which the writers all seemed to individually prepare. Though the greater song was continuous, I noticed the individual pillar readers occasionally paused so that the accompanying writer had time to close up a filled scroll and replace it with a fresh one. Whenever a scroll was filled, it was taken by one of the mighty eagles I had seen flying up toward the crown. When the writers laid aside a scroll, it was then picked up carefully, enclosed in the strong talons of one of the mighty raptors, and taken aloft and abroad to be delivered. None of the eagles delayed in their task; all seemed especially keen to bring forth the words that were given to them. After having heard the song, I felt I understood why.

It was directly that we were led through the archway of the first door, entering into a wide and open space were several servants of the house (similar in form to the readers and writers) came to offer refreshment. The servants each bowed low as the king greeted them by name; beautiful names in a tongue which I do not have the skill to accurately record. They appeared different from one another, though the servants were all dressed in raiment of a silvery blue hue. Their faces shone out like stars in the night, pleasant to look upon and not damaging to the eye. With soft, melodious voices they greeted us and attended to us by setting in our hands fine glasses that were filled with a rich, enlivening drink. As we sipped slowly from the cups, we found our alertness increased and any soreness in our limbs had receded (the hike to the house had been a considerable distance to traverse).

For some time, we milled about the room, observing the artistry which was so readily available. Warm were the walls, like the setting sun burnished in gold and yellow. They seemed to radiate from the dark wooden floors beneath our feet so in no place were we met by cold or bitterness. Betwixt the warmth exuding from the walls and the breeze running like a river through the entryway, we were left in a state of contentment. With a deep sigh, I looked up for the first time to see the ceiling of this room was painted to appear like the night sky. The warm colors of the walls were such that, as they moved upwards toward the ceiling, they darkened into purples and blues and other cool hues until it seemed as though one was looking into a clear sky at dusk. Most vibrant of all were the stars themselves, which twinkled and shone in a most realistic manner, much to my awe and amazement. Many there were, covering the broadness of the high ceiling, so that I could not have counted them all even had I stood there for several days.

"They call this room the Star Room," the king said, pointing toward the ceiling with his free hand.

"There are so many of them!" I replied, chirping with amazement. "How did they get them all up there?"

"It must have taken them *forever* to put them there," Hope said in agreement. All of the servants in the room began to chuckle at this and the king himself gave out a hearty laugh.

"No one 'put them there.' Rather each star represents the lifeforce of an individual. They appear here whenever the individual has been restored to their rightful place in creation," the king explained. Hope, who was staring at the ceiling with wide eyes suddenly pointed to an empty patch where two new stars were beginning to appear.

"Look!" she exclaimed. Dimly though they began, two new lights were beginning to glow brighter: one a cool silver and the other a warm gold.

"Those stars are us, aren't they?" I asked, turning my eyes to meet the king's kind face.

"Yes," he said simply "And they will shine brighter yet, still." And with that, we finished our glasses and were ushered into the next room.

Unlike the wide foyer we had just left, the next room was both narrower and longer in its design and contained few pieces of furniture so that it appeared to us as a great hallway leading from the house's entrance to many other rooms within. The first thing I noticed upon entering were the walls which were colored a searing crimson. This seemed to contrast well against the white marbled tiles that echoed the soft patter of bare feet as we walked across. I likely would have passed quickly through the arterial were it not for the intricate tapestries which hung along the wall. Each one was exquisite, laid out on golden cloth and embroidered with complex weavings that contained images. I saw a great many things as the walls were lined from top to bottom with hardly any space free. I began to walk slower so I could examine a few of them as we passed (which neither Hope nor the king seemed to mind).

The first one that caught my eye was of a kinglike figure sitting at a table with a quill, writing. Beside him was a harp which he appeared to be plucking as he jotted down notes on a parchment. It was his eyes that caught my attention; deeply set and full of emotion. I followed the tapestry with my own, taking in the story that was laid out. The following scene depicted this same king figure prostrate on the floor, weeping. In the next he laughed and danced and ran about the streets of a city. Then, he sat quietly beside a stream, listening to its soft babbling noises, taking joy in the tranquility of the moment. The dozens of scenes that came after showed an array of emotions, all carried out by the same man who, even as he ran, did not flee the depths of his emotions. Even as he hid himself away from the world, he did not close off his wellspring of a heart and prevent himself from experiencing the wide range it had to offer.

Another tapestry showed a woman in a throne room facing a ruler of great power. Even as her hands trembled, she did not shrink or back down when speaking her request. Yet another tapestry depicted a child running through a meadow with great joy. Several scenes later, that same meadow was depicted as a barren land touched deeply by the clawing hands of war. Even so, the ending scenes promised redemption. Story after story passed my gaze. Some depicted times long past, while others appeared more recent or even unfinished. Great pain was contained within, for the stories were true to the nature of life. Even as joy abounded in places, darkness seemed to bite at the edges in an attempt to taint each story as it was written. As we neared the end of the long hall, I felt my own emotions welling up. Just as I thought I would kneel down and submit myself to crying, I saw another tapestry.

Hanging above the archway of the next room was a tapestry wider than I had seen before. Many scenes were contained within: a mother with her babe, a child in a temple, a dusty man walking across the deserts from city to city. His followers grew in number as he went about teaching and healing. Then they shrank before him as he was taken and beaten before finally being left to hang on a tree. And then I saw *the lamb*. The same lamb I had seen time and again, lying wrapped in a shroud and sealed in a tomb. But the tomb could not be contained. In an elaborate display of light, the shroud was broken, and the lamb leapt to its feet where it transformed into the lion and ran headlong into the darkness that hung about the earth. It fought with the same fierceness that had broken the heart of the storm on the sea. And everywhere they went, they were depicted as heralds of redemption and champions of the light. Trumpets were shown sounding out so all who heard were notified of their coming. Still even more amazing, I found there, within the image of the lion and lamb, the same man who was shown in the earlier scenes, bloodied and spent. But here he went about, tall and strong, seeking the lost and the broken in every corner of the earth. No matter how far they were, he sought them. No matter how lost they became, he found them. No matter how broken they seemed, he healed them. And then I saw his face and it bore the likeness of the one who had found *me* stuck and decaying in a place far away from where I now was. It was then I understood for the first time since I had begun my journey, lying rusted on the long iron tracks. *The Lion and the Lamb and the Man were all one.*

My knees buckled under the weight of this truth and I collapsed to the ground in tears. Through my blurred vision I saw beside me that Hope had become overwhelmed as well. My head began to swirl as my heart pounded heavily in my sinking chest. Whether it was due to sorrow or joy that I became immobilized under the archway of the Crimson Hall, I could not tell. However, soon thereafter I was met with the sound of a familiar and soothing voice.

"Why do you cry, redeeméd ones?" the voice said, though it was not the king's. The voice came wafting through the archway like a warm breeze, pulling us toward it. "Come in so I can see you," it said gently.

The king then took us each by the hand and helped us to our feet. Then, with the careful guidance of a seasoned shepherd, he led us into the next room.

12

The One We Met

THE FIRST THING I noticed was the *light*, soft and pervasive. Even so, my eyes had trouble adjusting as Hope and I were led deliberately toward the soothing and familiar voice. Images of the restful valley resurfaced in my mind. The scent of the valley came pressing through my nostrils, more pungent even than when I had first encountered it. Then I felt a hand come reaching out to wipe the tears from eyes and I saw. There before me stood the Creator in all his wonder and majesty. Behind him was a rather large and homely chair where he sat planted like a mountain, steady and unwavering. In his arms were righteousness and justice, which he exercised with precision. In his fingers flowed creativity. Nimbly, I saw him working a needle in his right hand, sewing a tapestry that lay strewn across his lap. The scenes which I saw embroidered matched the style of those in the Crimson Hall and I suddenly understood it was the Creator who had made them all.

When he breathed, life flew out of his nostrils and filled the room. And as I looked around, I saw for the first time that the room was packed with green things. Flowers and vines sprouted from the floor and coiled about the foot of the Creator's chair. A spring bubbled up from the floor beside the Creator's chair, watering the room. But when I looked upon his face I suddenly found myself gazing into a deep well. In his eyes could be seen an expanse greater than all of the universe, and it was filled to the brim with love.

"Welcome," the Creator said speaking from his seat. "I am glad you are here. Come and stand beside me. There is something I want to show you."

After he had said this, he extended an arm to Hope and me and bade us come and stand at his side. Once I was standing at his left and Hope at his right, he unraveled the golden tapestry and showed us the scenes that were embroidered therein.

"This is the story of two strong individuals," he began in a deep voice. "Long ago, before time began, I desired to fashion two beautiful lights in the darkness."

He pointed to a golden star and a silver one sewn into the dark blue thread of the first scene. The creator had placed them there after carefully crafting them, like a jeweler carving two precious stones.

"I named them," he continued, "and thus filled them with life. Hope and Courage I called them, for I have promised they will prevail over the icy cold of Fear. Fear is their greatest enemy, a force which bites at the edges of all worthy creatures, nibbling at their inner strength."

He showed us in the scenes that followed where the stars dimmed and grew colder, till naught but sparks remained.

"It is true that hope sometimes dims, and courage fades. But they can never go out entirely, because I have set them together."

He pointed to their adjacent positioning, signifying the partnership which he had created for them.

"Together, their lifeforces feed one another, shining light even in the midst of the deepest darkness. I am saying this to you both now because it is important you know what I have promised for you. You are never alone."

He then continued to show us the story, though the setting had changed markedly from the start. The stars were now people wandering about the Earth, looking for people to encourage. As they went, they were followed by a dark figure that was depicted always in the corners of each scene, waiting to make his move.

And we observed as the figure wore down the strength of both Hope and Courage until they each stopped to rest, apart from one another. Slowly, each fell asleep on the pathway that had been set before them and time began to pass. There it was that Fear whispered in their ear.

You are not alive; you are made of iron and of stone. You cannot move from this place.

Over and over he repeated these words until they believed them, and their flesh was changed from human to cold steel. But they were not transformed into rocks, but rather locomotives, and the pathway was turned to rails.

I interrupted the Creator's story at this point to ask a question, "Why was it that we became locomotives, of all things? Why did we not turn into a tree, or a hill, or a simply a statue of ourselves?"

The Creator turned to look at me with a wise expression and answered, "Fear cannot change the nature of created things. It convinced you you were made of steel rather than flesh, but your nature is to be an object that moves, not one that is fixed."

"So, we were never really engines?" Hope asked.

"No," answered the Creator. "Nor was your pathway actually a railroad. It simply took a while to uproot those lies, and an attentive guide to help you believe," he then gestured to the one who had been our Engineer, though we now understood his true identity was of far greater importance.

"As soon as those lies became settled, I sent him out to find you and bring you here so you might remember who you are."

He then drew us around to the front of his chair and sat us at his feet.

"Listen," he commanded gently but firmly. "You are children of a promise; my promise. I will not allow the darkness to corrupt your hearts. You are children of one who loves you more than you know. You are children of the one who set the stars in the sky and planted the trees that grow from the Earth. I am sending you out into the world, not alone but together. Together you will be lights to the world, encouraging those who despair and inspiring those who fear."

"Can we not stay?" I asked, pleading with the Creator. "Everything has been so clear since I came to this place."

Both the Creator and the king smiled wide at this request.

"You will stay, eventually," the king said, patting me reassuringly on the shoulder. "Now is a time for growth, and all created things have a part to play in this. As stars in the sky, you will be mirrors of a sort, reminding those who look up that there is a greater light."

The Creator then got up from his seat and bent down to embrace us both. It was a moment so gracious and full it seemed to go on without end and linger for a long time after. He then turned to each of us offering final words.

To Hope he said, "Remember there is an ending to your story. It ends in righteousness; a path where things are restored. Hope defiantly."

He then patted her gently on the head and wiped the last solitary tear from her cheek.

Turning to me, he paused and looked discerningly at my face. "Do not be afraid of time," he said after a moment had passed. "I have given you all that you will need and then some. I know you love to watch the green things of the world and cherish all that is good. Know however, that nothing is lost forever. Take courage in your heart."

He then bent his head so his forehead met mine for a minute, hugged me once more, and returned to his seat.

"Go now from this place, together," he said finally. "Your time on Earth is not over. I will call you here again."

I then took Hope's hand in my own and we were ushered out of the Creator's room. I turned back once to see the Creator smiling widely, his fingers moving once again on the tapestry in his lap. Our tapestry. Once we were out of the house, the king then stopped and turned to face us both.

"I'm afraid this is where I must leave you as well. You weren't the only ones who found themselves stuck."

He winked at us both as he said this. He then pointed to the side of Elon opposite from where we had come up.

"That is the direction you both must head."

He then added, "Don't be afraid of getting lost, if that happens. I'll come find you."

He then squeezed both of our hands tightly in his own and turned to walk back across the plateau toward the side we had come up. We stood there for a while watching him as he went. Eventually he came to where the mists covered the descent and as he walked down, melding with the fog, for a moment I saw him don his greasy engineer's cap once more. Off he went to find another lost engine, stuck somewhere on the long iron tracks.

My friend Hope and I then walked toward the opposite end of Elon where the sun was rising high. No mists clouded the pathway which wound gently down the slope, allowing us to see for some distance. It was far out on the horizon that we saw it: a dark cloud hovering about a tiny house, with a pathway leading right to its doorstep. My heart began to beat faster at the sight.

"Don't be afraid," said Hope gripping my hand tighter. "We'll do this together."

I suddenly felt relieved to have such a friend at my side. I took a moment to remember the words of the Creator and then we set out down the mountainside, away from the Great House by the lake where the Creator sat weaving, and down into the valley below to face the darkness.

And we were not alone.